Feeling the Hurt,

Healing the Heart

Marie Carroll

PublishAmerica
Baltimore

ISBN: 1-4137-5155-5
PUBLISHED BY PUBLISHAMERICA, LLLP
www.publishamerica.com
Baltimore

Printed in the United States of America

I give special thanks to those individuals who made the writing of this book possible.

The Beginning

It all began some years ago when I found the empty ring box in some junk in the basement. Perhaps I should have done more at the time than write a silly letter to him. Knowing you can't go back, it's best to simply try hard to move ahead, no matter how difficult.

The missing birthstone ring was supposedly for someone who celebrates a different birthday than mine. This was my first of many clues that all was not well in my belief that this person I've loved with all my heart shared his time, money, and affection with someone else.

The aforementioned letter gave him every opportunity to explain his strange behavior, tell me our marriage was over, or tell me whatever was on his mind. He stated that all was well with us. He knew or loved no other. Thus he forfeited this first opportunity to be honest and forged ahead with something that almost destroyed us both.

I continued to have faith in our relationship and faith in his words to me. One simply believes what they have to in order to look at the world and their live in a sane way. We've all heard it said before—"What you don't know, won't hurt you."

I have always been a religious person, having served my church and God in whatever way I could use my talents. During this period of my life I was extremely active in my church. I typed the worship service bulletin, sang in the choir, served on Administrative Council and served on numerous committees. I was also the church treasurer. I usually went to church alone and would then visit my parents each week, as they lived by my church.

From that time until now many things have transpired to us both. Sometimes shortly after writing the letter I began experiencing anxiety attacks and bouts of depression. Who can ever explain why this happens? Could it have been the fact that I realized I was probably losing him—or perhaps it was a major health concern I had at that time. Needless to say, it was one of the hardest times of my life. Oh, he was always positive that I would be fine. Always upbeat and trying so hard to be helpful. But these years later, I find this was at the beginning of his secret life with the receiver of "the ring."

Lies

He worked so much overtime then—a special project at work. Naturally, I wanted to believe him and so I did. How many nights I would just sit and cry because I was so depressed and anxious. I couldn't watch the television, couldn't read, I could hardly function through the day at work. Often I would leave and go for a ride just to escape the fear I was dwelling in. But nights were much more difficult. I remember just standing outside in our yard sobbing. I didn't want to be alone!

I hated weekends. I am not sure why that is so. He worked— or so he said—every Saturday. On Sunday he would always "have some running to do"—meet some guys for breakfast or go to work to check things out, etc.

For several reasons I stopped attending church around this time period. I would escape as early as I could from the house. Saturday would find me walking around the local mall crying softly to myself. Sunday I would be out searching for houses. I had a need to move at that time as I realized my husband lost all interest in our home. I wasn't sure why. Wasn't he feeling well or was he just tired of being "Mr. Fixit"?

Sometimes he humored me and occasionally even went to look at houses I had found. I honestly believed we could just move to our future home that needed no repairs and that would fix everything.

Questions and No Answers

Why did he suddenly start going to work a different way — almost twice as long as the usual way? Was he really working so much overtime? If so why wasn't there more money? How many times do you have to run out for cigarettes, gas or ice cream, when you could have gotten those items on the way home? How is it he suddenly needs to share breakfast with some friends on Sunday morning? How come he has to go back to work so many times to check things? What things?

All this Christmas shopping, who is it for? Is he really impotent or just not interested in me anymore? Why can't he spend time with me when I feel I'm losing my mind because I'm so scared and lonesome? When he is with me the television is much more important. Why won't he even talk to me?

Does he not like this home that we built so lovingly together fifteen years ago? If so, why doesn't he care about it like he used to?

Why must I go everywhere by myself? Weddings, family functions, etc? Oh, sometimes he would meet me there but more often than not, he begged off with one excuse or another. Why couldn't he join me when I traveled out of state to visit our son and family? I was sure he loved those lovely little grandchildren!

Do you suppose I live on another planet? How naïve can one get when you wish to not acknowledge the frightfully obvious?

Does God Only Give You What You Can Handle?

My life at this junction was a mess. My father was not well and my mother needed much more help than I could possibly give her. My brother was going through a divorce and his children refused to see him. My sister was experiencing severe depression and had to be hospitalized. My sister-in-law was diagnosed with breast cancer, my favorite aunt died from uterine cancer, and my son and daughter-in-law, who had previously moved to another state, had two miscarriages.

We had legal problems regarding my aunt's will. To make matters worse, my own physical health was unstable because of my having breast cancer seven years prior. I was having a gallbladder problem which was promptly diagnosed as liver cancer. I had plural effusion and nodules on my liver. I found that after previously having cancer that all my doctors were only too content to assume the cancer was back.

The emergency room doctor told me quite calmly that my cancer was back and it was in my liver and lungs. I was overwhelmed—I had been given a death sentence! I was happy that my own children were grown and had their own families. However, I began to feel horribly sad about not ever seeing my grandchildren again.

I felt so alone because of my husband's working so many hours overtime. I ate alone, and I sat alone at night and became more anxious. The best way to describe my fear was that I had a feeling of some horrible thing hanging around me waiting to destroy me. I felt terrified! I just cried and cried and felt I was losing my mind.

I remember vividly how I hated getting up in the morning. I woke up most mornings at four o'clock with severe stomach cramps. Naturally I thought this was part of the cancer symptoms. Every ache and pain I had I attributed to cancer.

After I did get up in the morning I would start off to work but would stop several times on my way because I felt so sick to my stomach. When I got to work I would cry if someone talked to me. I was sure it became obvious to anyone who worked with me that something was terribly wrong.

I became super paranoid. I couldn't watch commercials on television about hospitals and illness. Each time the phone rang, I would have an anxiety attack. Days at work were terribly stressful. I am a secretary by profession and needless to say the phone rang quite often.

The second week in December, I had a needle aspiration to remove the fluid from my lung. Two days later the doctor called to inform us that the plural effusion was nothing to worry about and the nodules in my liver were hepatic cysts caused by the medicine I had taken for breast cancer. I was told to go for additional scans in three months, but I never returned. I decided that hospitals and doctors were beneficial to some people, but I wouldn't be among them for some time. I had developed "white coat phobia."

It took quite some time to pull myself together and become relatively normal once again. I began to see a psychiatrist back then. I had to at least try to come to a reality of what was happening to me.

Right from the beginning the doctor suggested that things weren't as great in our marriage as I portrayed. He stated my husband wouldn't be working so much overtime if he were truly concerned about my well being. Naturally that upset me! How dare he tell me I didn't have a good marriage! Why we never fought or argued. I knew we loved each other.

But even then I knew the problem; even if I couldn't admit it to myself, my husband had interests elsewhere

After ten visits and two thousand dollars I stopped my visits to the psychiatrist. He certainly wasn't helping me—just upsetting me more. Each time I went he continuously rehashed all of what he thought should be my concerns. I didn't need to hear from an outside source that this guy I married wasn't totally focused on me. I was hearing it much too often in my subconscious. I did, however, get help from the medicine that he prescribed for me. It was very difficult for me to take the medicine because I didn't want to become "addicted." Also, I felt that I was not in control if I had to rely on medicine to survive on a daily basis.

I began to realize that I might be having some unconscious dreams early in the morning to make me so uncomfortable. The mornings continued to be bad. I felt terrible, but refused to take time off of work because I didn't want to be alone. I worked in a school and was terrified if school would be cancelled because of inclement weather. I just wouldn't stay home alone anymore than I had to.

One day I felt really lousy. I stayed home, but felt so scared being home alone. I felt like I had to have company so I turned on the television. I saw a talk show with Dr. Wayne Dwyer as a guest speaker. He told a story about the "black hole in the sidewalk." It went as follows:

DAY 1—I walked down the street. There was a big black hole in the sidewalk. I fell in it and couldn't get out. It wasn't my fault. I was there for a very long time.

DAY 2 - I walked down the street. There was a big black hole in the sidewalk. I fell in it again. I can't believe this! It wasn't my fault. It still took a long time to get out.

DAY 3—I walked down the street. There was a big black hole in the sidewalk. I saw it, but I still fell in it anyway! I believe it was my fault. I got out right away.

DAY 4—I walked down the street. There was a big black hole in the sidewalk. I walked around it.

DAY 5—I walked down a different street.

This little story changed my life. It really spoke to me. I began to see that I was my own worst enemy. I showered and went off to work. This was the beginning of my emerging from where I had been (my black hole or self-pity, anxiety and terror.)

My best friend was my savior at this time. She supplied me with endless hours of listening, self help books, and meditation tapes. I would listen to the tapes on the way to work and back.

It was a long trip out of my black hole. I worked extremely hard but finally dug my way back to sanity.

Stress 101

Shortly after I had come back from my dark period, our oldest son told us he was getting divorced and filing for custody of his two children. He was horribly depressed and I promptly threw myself into helping him in any way that I possibly could. I simply couldn't have him slipping into where I had gone

My best friend's son had committed suicide because of depression and I knew how much my son was like her son. He told his brother that he planned to just work and work until all his bills were paid and then he could just die. It broke my heart!

In the beginning both he and his ex-wife were granted shared custody. However, his ex-wife was not happy about this and tried in every manner possible to prove that my son and his family were unfit. The children, then six and seven, along with their dad moved in with us.

I was accused of bathing with them, giving them drugs, doing voodoo and other things. I became the enemy or "other woman" because I let them move in. His ex-wife told me she wanted him ruined and in the gutter and I saved him. I was, in her eyes, the enemy!

Our life once again became turbulent. Disturbing phone calls and messages, visits to my place of employment—where she would go from the extreme of begging me to help her win him back and in seconds change and become disrespectful and downright nasty.

Life was unpredictable during this period. I tried very hard to support my son and his decision. I would often go on day trips to parks, the zoo, and museum, etc. with my son and the grandchildren. We were often running off to play miniature golf, the movies and going out to eat. My husband never seemed to want to join us as he continued to work overtime and just didn't seem available.

Up to this time I had always been so concerned about planning my life around my husband and trying to be home while he was there so we could spend time together. I think I gave up after my severe bout of depression as I knew I had to think about me. Also, I felt my son and grandchildren needed me more than he did at this time.

Six months after my son's divorce, my husband was diagnosed with prostate cancer. Naturally, the whole family was once again quite upset. After several doctor visits we decided to go out of the area for a relatively different treatment. I spent countless hours searching the internet for the appropriate doctor and hospital where we would both feel comfortable having this procedure performed. All seemed to go as well as we expected, but there were some troubling after effect. We weathered this storm together much like we did my breast cancer years before.

We made several trips out of town to see his specialist. I traveled with him for all but one visit. I began to notice he seemed withdrawn and put up a private screen around himself. I felt somewhat hurt and shut out but attributed it to his feeling helpless during this time, so I once again made those little excuses for his behavior and moved on.

I did however, realize that I had not been as attentive to him and vowed to change that. I once again had that stark realization of how precious every moment of life is and felt God would take care of my son and grandchildren, but my husband now needed my time and care. Despite my husband's illness he still insisted on working as much overtime as possible.

Death of Parents and Confession

The next trauma we faced was my husband's mother passed away while she was sitting at the table writing bills. He was contacted at work and told me when he came home. This was a hash reality to us both, because my mother-in-law and I had been close friends. I would really miss her!

She had heart by-pass surgery several years ago and it really seemed like a miracle that she was still so active and very much a part of everyone's life. As odd as it seemed one of the first things that went through my head when my husband informed me of his mother's passing was *now he will tell me about his secret life*.

Two weeks later, on a Saturday, I was planning on going shopping. I guessed my husband would be spending the day once again at work. However, he was very quiet and seemed disturbed. When I was ready to go out the door he asked me if we could talk. He stated that he had something important to tell me and he knew I would be upset.

To say my heart stopped momentarily would be an understatement. I was sure his cancer was back and had traveled to another part of his body.

I sat on the sofa next to him as he told me he had been unfaithful. My reaction was, "Is that all! I thought you were going to die!"

He replied, "I should have." He stated that he had planned to commit suicide rather than tell me and hurt me so terribly. I saw his torture and forgot about my own pain. I immediately became his caretaker, telling him just about anything he needed to hear to make it all right once again.

I felt that I was "outside myself" and was simply not facing my real feelings during this time. Looking back, I feel that I actually was looking down on the scene as it unfolded. I remember feeling his pain and became aware of the seriousness of his self-hatred.

I was determined to help him through this before I could even dream of handling my feelings. I put all thoughts of myself on hold and refused to "go there" until I was ready emotionally and felt he was ready to face life once again.

We both cried and talked throughout that day. He saying what a horrible person he was and how everyone would hate him for the rest of his life and he deserved it.

We didn't talk much about "the other person" that day. It didn't seem important then. I was more concerned about his self-hatred and depression and vowed to do everything I could to help him. Later it became obvious, that I subconsciously reasoned that if I became busy with his care I could forget about my pain.

I told him no one needed to know about what had happened. He didn't seem to care because he said his life was over. He could never respect himself again. He was extremely concerned about how our sons would hate him. Through tears he spoke about how proud his mother and father must be of the son they raised.

It was indeed a long day. We both couldn't eat and were exhausted. Toward evening he said he was going to leave briefly to go for cigarettes. After his being gone for thirty minutes, he called from work and said he wouldn't be home that night. He said that he knew that I hated him and he felt I needed to not be around him at the time. I told him that wasn't so and begged him to come home. He said he would sleep on the sofa at work. He said he would be fine and I didn't have to worry about him again. He was crying again as he hung up.

That night became a nightmare. I tired to call him back and he wouldn't answer. I envisioned him killing himself in any way imaginable. I called my sister and sobbed out the whole story to her. She felt as helpless as I did. Next I called my son who lives in another state. He tried to call his dad at work to talk to him, but also got no response. I became more upset for having caused others to share my worry and confusion.

I sobbed throughout the night. The anguish I felt was indescribable. When my tears were spent, I sat in our living room and just waited for the police to come to the door to tell me they had found my husband and he was dead. Our dog sat by the door and wanted to go outside. I remember how my legs wouldn't work to help her and I didn't care.

My husband came home around eight o'clock that morning. I was upset and angry. I told him what he did by staying away through the night was worse than his being unfaithful. The anger I began to feel brought forth some questions that were not important the day before.

I found that his "being unfaithful" went on for more than three years. This "other person" lives down the road from us and I don't know her. She is a year older than me and very needy. She suffers from back pain and other health issues and because of her being unhealthy, she can't get a full-time job.

He met her in a doughnut shop, where she is still employed part-time. He told me that when he quit smoking a few years ago, he met her and started smoking again. This was another reason to dislike her! He informed me that she is a nice person and "a lady."

I became angry and stated, "Any women that sleeps with someone's husband is not a lady and you would be wise to never refer to her with that title again in my presence."

Our talking, crying and not eating continued throughout that day. Some things were discussed and others were not. My husband didn't have a clue why this happened. He claimed it just happened! He stated that he loves us both and is very confused. He said he wanted our marriage to survive but was uncertain if I could ever forgive him and thus continue loving him.

He was feeling somewhat better when he went off to work the next day. I look back on this day and think I was feeling this was all a bad dream. There were periods of reality and tears and moments of unbelief. I lasted the day at work probably because I was in shock. The next day I needed to stay home from work and throw myself into some serious house cleaning, hoping to chase all thoughts of the last few days from my betrayed soul.

He called sometime that afternoon and seemed rather pleased. He stated, "I hate so much leaving her now. She is having a lot of problems. They are turning off her power and her phone and gas because she can't afford it. She will probably lose her home and she isn't well."

He added that he thought he would feel much better about all of this if he could just give her some money to see her through this bad time of his leaving her.

Now we didn't just have money hanging around. Without giving this much thought I felt, hey, if this is what it takes for him to begin to feel good about himself, I'm all for it!

Together we searched avenues to obtain "the money." We contemplated borrowing the money from our charge card, but the interest was extremely high. The only way it was available was though an annuity left to me by my aunt. He said he would finish renovating his car and after selling it we would put the money back in the annuity.

The deed was done! He called her to let her know that the money was put into her bank account. He told her that he had sold his antique car and that was how he obtained the money.

I suppose it wouldn't have looked good to tell her, "Here is some money for you to get by, it's from my wife."

It was not a small amount. I truly couldn't believe she accepted it. My mind screamed *What kind of woman is this?* I think that stunned me almost as much as this whole story thus far.

Also, I was displeased that he had access to her bank account. Why?

Three days later he borrowed more money and asked a friend to give it to her and tell her she won it on a lottery ticket. He told me about this additional money later that evening. I was naturally upset! I began to get a bad feeling about this as I started to wonder *how much would be enough to ease his guilt.*

Approaching Holidays

Thanksgiving was one week later. My husband told me that before "his confession," he had promised "his friend" that he would stop to feed her dog and cats while she visited her daughter out of town. He said he tried to contact one of her friends to do this but had no success.

We were to travel to his sister's home for a family dinner. That was the day I learned where "she" lived. We stopped by her house on the way to my sister-in-law's home. I waited in the car crying. I was stunned by the fact that her house was only four miles down the road from us. How very convenient!

He sarcastically said as we left her house, "I can just imagine you telling about how you spent Thanksgiving—oh, we stopped by my husband's girlfriend's house to feed her pets on the way to my sister-in-laws."

It was a sad time—we traveled on to his sister's home to have dinner. Neither of us wanted to eat and we both did a fair job of putting on a happy smile. I'm sure if my mother-in-law hadn't passed away so recently, we would have had to explain our strange, sad moods.

Later that night I went to my parents' home to visit. My husband stayed home because he wasn't feeling well. I think it would have been very difficult for him to face everyone even though they knew nothing about what had happened. It was very hard to act cheerful but I became very good at acting during that period.

Christmas came and went. He gave me a beautiful silver

heart necklace with a loving inscription on the back as a Christmas gift. However, we were like two strangers living together. I began to feel that I didn't really know this person I was married to. He certainly wasn't the same person I fell in love with thirty-three years ago. We would spend nights watching television and not really communicating. He still was going outside for long periods of time. I was super concerned because I knew how badly he was suffering yet.

I believe I spent the first six months in shock. The whole thing truly didn't reach the logical part of my brain. I was too concerned about his welfare and state of mind and really forgot about me.

I recall visiting his doctor, without an appointment. I waited two hours before I finally got to speak to him. I had to tell his doctor how depressed he was and why. I felt I needed someone to help me with his state of mind. His doctor scheduled an appointment for my husband and after speaking to him prescribed an anti-depression medication. He did advise that we should both seek counseling, but after talking with my husband about this, I knew he would never agree.

I became very curious about this other person. Maybe this is only a female thing—but I wondered, what did she look like? Was she thinner and prettier than me? I knew she was somewhat older, but perhaps she had a great personality and they had a great time together. Maybe they had a lot of mutual friends. She probably made great meals for him. I didn't even want to think about the sex issues! I just felt that I was lacking in every area I could imagine.

My self image took another downward spiral when I discovered that I had developed basal cell skin cancer on my face during this period. I had two lesions that the doctor had to remove, and repair. This resulted in an incision from my left inner eyebrow down the side of my nose and across my cheek. The surgery left me with two back eyes and numerous stitches that took some time to heal. It was around this time that my hair started to fall out. My beautician kept telling me my hair was getting thinner and thinner. I kept imagining myself bald and wondered what could possibly happen next!

My husband continued to be quiet and moody, but I attributed this to separation anxiety from his friend, the continuation of his severe depression and his continued low self-esteem.

There was a period of time, after watching a movie on television that I became convinced he was going to kill me. This thought occurred to me because the movie had such a scene in it. He treated me like I was made of glass, never nasty, always very nice but too polite. He behaved as though we were strangers, which hurt my already bruised feelings. He was way too polite and this really bothered me.

I know now that he would have never done such a thing, but at that time I wasn't thinking about anything very rationally. I became convinced I was a terrible wife and mother. I was sure that the world would be better off if I just disappeared. I can honestly say that I wasn't suicidal, but I simply didn't care if I lived or died. I became careless, in fact reckless at times. I thought I won't kill myself, but I certainly tempted fate to shorten my life on many occasions.

At this time I began to keep a journal about my feelings. They weren't very nice at times but the journaling helped immensely. The hate poured out, not only for this situation but mostly for myself and the useless person I thought I had become.

The pity party began! My life as I thought of it was a huge lie! All my future dreams disappeared! I was in a constant state of devastation. I was wounded and wanted to die. I remember the hours of severe pain and no amount of crying eased it. I was set assail on an unfamiliar ocean with only part of a boat. This person I trusted more than anyone in the world has betrayed me! These thoughts took up most of my waking hours.

Then the pain was internalized. The rejection I felt caused my self-esteem to completely disappear. I realized I had to come to terms with these feelings or I would be permanently scarred. I felt isolated from everyone and everything. I would look at people where ever I went and wonder if they too had been betrayed or had betrayed someone. I became pre-occupied with "what ifs" and "whys."

It became very difficult to sleep. I can remember not wanting any physical contact with my husband. Some evenings, I would take a comforter and sleep on the floor or go to another part of the house to sleep. He would usually come looking for me and talk me into coming back to bed. I really loved him so much! How could you love someone so much and hate them at the same time? Maybe I am crazy. That's it! No wonder he went searching for someone else!

Sometime later, on a Friday morning before work, my husband seemed extremely distracted. He left thirty minutes earlier than usual. I had gotten in the habit of watching which way he left in the morning and came home at night. I now knew where she lived and could ascertain when he left if he would be going past her house. This particular morning he went, what I perceived, as "the wrong way." I immediately became suspicious and followed him.

It was mid January and there was snow on the ground that day as I drove by her house and found his truck in her driveway. Tears wouldn't come! Did I cry them all out already? Surely not! I parked the car across the street, walked over to her house on shaky legs and sat in the snow by his truck and sobbed. My heart cried out, *what does this mean?* I felt lost and I was sure all was hopeless. I went back to my car and started to go back home. I couldn't see very well through the tears that finally came, but I didn't really care.

Perhaps they are going away somewhere. I began to think. *I need to tell him goodbye!* I promptly turned around, drove back to her house, parked the car and went to her front door. I began to knock—timidly at first. I heard a dog bark from inside and thought, well the dog will let them know someone is out here.

But no one answered.

I began to knock much louder until finally after ten minutes I was out of control and I was just beating on the door. But still no one answered, even though by now the dog was also making quite a racket.

I had such an utter sense of hopelessness. I sank down on the porch and sobbed. I finally pulled my self together and got up and left. I got back to my car and made it back to my home in record time. I was again sobbing.

For some odd reason when I arrived home my priority beside packing and leaving was the jewelry my husband had given to me. I began to take all the jewelry out and laid it all neatly out on the bed. I then ran and got my suitcase and frantically began to pack my things.

It wasn't long before my husband came home. The rage and hurt just poured out of me. I told him to take all that jewelry and give it to her, to give her all of our money and to bring her to our home to live, because I was leaving and that was all she really wanted.

I don't know why or when I finally calmed down. I finally gave in and listened to what he had to say, maybe because I was so drained. He stated that he had just gone to see if she was alright, that nothing happened. They were both right inside the door crying while I was knocking, but didn't answer. He begged me to give him time to get over this, that he truly wanted our marriage to work. He was just so concerned about her future and the fact that he felt he had ruined her life. He claimed he had a lot of thinking to do. I told him I would leave our home for awhile to give him time to get his thoughts in order. He vehemently disagreed!

I sometimes looked back at this period of time and wished that I had just walked away without anymore scars. But one never knows what the future holds and I guess it was just fate that made me stay and continue on this crazy journey of patching our life.

Had I known then that I would maybe have had piece of mind in the future I would have been more tempted to disappear. At this time in my life I was more concerned about his welfare and my broken heart and spirit. I felt he was the only one who could fix them. Little did I know there was much more hurt on the way!

Moving Out/Deciding What to Do?

A few days later my husband decided to go to his parents' empty house to stay for a few days to get his thoughts in order. He told me he knew he wanted to finish his life as my husband, but he had to think about a lot of things. He called me several times each day and night. After being gone for four nights he came home and told me he wanted more than anything in the world to stay with me. He also promised to never communicate with "her" again. Yes I had heard that before, but oh how I wanted to believe him and I also wanted our marriage to work.

Could it be that this may work after all? He certainly seemed much different. However, he still refused to talk much about why this happened and what actually did happen. I would get little tidbits of information every now and then but nothing to appease my curious mind. Each time I wanted to talk or ask a question, it usually brought on tears from us both. I decided these episodes weren't worth it.

I began to see a counselor by myself. We worked on some issues about my past that made me realize that a lot of my present insecurities were founded in my early years and my fear of being abandoned. We made a lot of progress and she finally declared I didn't need to continue to meet with her.

Three weeks later my husband was by my side when my father passed away. Our whole family stayed at our home throughout those sad days. Things were a little stressed between our two sons and their dad, but I knew it would take some time for everything to fall into place as it once was. I felt that my husband was truly back and much more attentive than he had been in years. Perhaps, there was hope for us after all.

My only real fear was the knowledge that my husband still had deep feelings for this other woman. Despite his loving attitude, the seeds of distrust had been planted. It seemed that with his getting better, I took on the depression.

I drove past her house endlessly, so I knew what kind of car she had. I began to search for her car at all the doughnut shops within a twenty mile radius to find out where she worked. On weekends I would follow him to work to see if that was where he was truly going. There were days I would park on a side street to just watch if he went by. I would then know which way he was going and be able to follow him more closely to see if he was going anywhere besides work.

Then one day I found "the doughnut shop." It was almost right under my nose. So close to home! I went through the drive through window and ordered a cup a coffee. "She" waited on me. I knew that she didn't know who I was. She was very pleasant. I noticed that she had a necklace on, much like the one he had given me the past Christmas. My first thought was, maybe two for the price of one!

I drove away crying. I pulled over after driving around for some time and called my husband at work. I told him I hadn't gone to work and that I had gone for coffee where "his friend" works and I had gone to the drive-in window and "she" had waited on me.

I said, "She was wearing a nice necklace. It looked like the one you gave me for Christmas this past year. Were you able to purchase two for the price of one?" I hung up and drove home. I felt justified being nasty!

He left work and came home to talk. He said he got the necklace for her a year or two ago. He confessed that he had bought her many gifts but always felt terribly guilty afterward because he felt that he was stealing money from me.

I realized that during these periods of time when we were

both so upset, he would open up and tell me things he previously kept from me. So I knew this was a good time for the questions again.

I asked him if she ever went with him for his check up for his prostate cancer.

He replied, "Yes, but she didn't go to the hospital with me, but traveled with me and visited her daughter who lives in the same town."

These little revelations hurt more than words can say and I wondered what else he didn't tell me. Now each time we would go to his doctors out of town, I would wonder, did they eat there? Did they stop here? This made me very uncomfortable to accompany him on any trip. I also began to think of his truck as "her truck," and if we went anywhere it was usually in my car.

My seeing her at her place of work just led to more questions and more anxiety. Questions I had no answers to. I increasingly knew it was important for us both to go for marriage counseling. I continued to plead with him to come with me to a good counselor, but he still refused.

The Beginning—of What?

The winter drug on that year but finally spring arrived. The new plants popping up and robins coming back — gave me new hope for a future. Despite all my detective work, I hadn't been able to ascertain if my husband was still in contact with "her."

One spring day I was feeling particularly cheerful as I removed the mail from our mailbox. In the mail was an envelope addressed to my husband. It tuned out to be a wedding invitation to "her" friend's wedding. It stated that he and a guest were invited to attend. I guess she was hoping for my husband to accompany her. My husband and I were both upset. He said he would not be attending and he would speak to the intended groom, whom he knew.

I responded by saying "Mr. (...) and his wife would not be attending."

A few days later I received the following message on my cell phone.

"You don't know me, but I am "her" daughter. I really wish you would tell your husband to leave my mom alone. He has been harassing her and she doesn't want anything to do with him. Tell him to finally make up his mind about whom he wants to be with, my mom or you."

Of course another scene developed. He stating that there positively had not been any contact. He said she probably put her daughter up to that because she was mad that he wasn't going to attend the wedding with her. What do I believe now? Is this never going to go away?

After that day, I would come home from work to find articles that my husband had given "her" thrown in our yard. I began to feel somewhat afraid of "her." I also sensed he was becoming concerned for my safety.

By this time I was really vigilant in my detective work. During this time I hardly slept at all. I would just lie awake and think.

One morning at two o'clock, I decided to search his truck. I quietly got up, searched his pockets for his truck keys and went outside in the rain. I found a cell phone that I had never seen and a package of condoms in the dash. I immediately went in and woke him. With the rage I felt, I don't know why I didn't become physically violent. He begged me to be calm so he could at least explain

He said the phone was from his place of employment. That it didn't work. He had it to try to fix it. He had the condoms at work, more or less to hide them from me while the affair was in full bloom. He just recently put them in his truck to get rid of them.

I asked, "Why did you have them, when 'she' is too old to become pregnant, or are you now seeing a younger person?"

He replied, "My doctor told me to use them because of my radio-active seed implant after the prostate surgery." But what I heard him say was—he was so concerned about her and her health and simply couldn't jeopardize her by leaving her with a radio-active seed.

Thus the rage began! The rage was my turning point in this horrible process when I began to realize this wasn't my fault at all. How naïve I'd been to blame myself! It was time to reverse the rejection and stop taking all of the blame for our failed relationship. I began to put the blame where I thought it belonged. I knew now who had caused this pain. Why it was this "other person!" You see, even then, I had difficulty being angry at my husband and held most of it to be "her" fault.

To say I was obsessing about "her" would be an

understatement. I would constantly go over in my mind all that had transpired. I searched his truck on several occasions and even his wallet. One night I found in his wallet a bank receipt for money deposited in her account. It was dated prior to his revelation about his secret life. Again he had plausible excuses for what he had in his possession. It was getting harder and harder to accept his excuses and I am not sure why I continued to do it.

On another spy mission I couldn't find his truck keys. He usually kept them in his jeans pocket, this night they weren't there. I thought, *where would he put them so I wouldn't notice anything unusual?* I checked his boots and sure enough the keys were there.

The next morning I told him that it was indeed strange for him to keep his truck keys in his boots. He must be hiding something. He said no, he had nothing to hide, he just didn't want me to be any more upset than I already was.

I would constantly try to convince him that we needed to talk about why this all happened. It was like talking to a rock—he wouldn't budge.

I began to stay up most of the night during this period. I would spend endless hours writing all my dark feelings in my journal and then reading it over and over. In my mind, I would go back to the day he confessed and think about that time to see if it still hurt as bad as it used to. I began to drink wine so I would be able to sleep for just an hour or two because I needed to function at work the next day.

I would wander endlessly around the house looking for a place that I felt safe from being hurt again. Then the time came when the wine didn't help me sleep any more. I began to drink whiskey or anything stronger. I would usually wake up with a headache, so I began to take pain pills along with the whiskey. I really didn't care about anything. I was just looking for numbness! I was tempting fate to just deal with me as it saw fit.

I remembered one particular night. I felt like I really hit the bottom. I thought of myself as a little bluebird, sitting on a barbed-wire fence, not knowing whether to fly away or just to fall onto the snowy ground and die. That image stayed with me for days.

I had such a need to cry! I would think of how much I missed my dad and my mother-in-law and wonder why this had happened. Didn't we have a good marriage? What did I do to make him that unhappy to find comfort in another's arms? Why wouldn't he answer my questions? I had 500 pieces to a 1,000 piece puzzle, and no picture to guide me. How could I heal and make this all better if I didn't know what was broken?

My husband felt the more I knew about his affair the worse I would feel. We had countless arguments about this. I tried to make him understand that it was much like the cancer that affected us both. It would continue to fester and would never heal until I could understand the story of it and get rid of it. I needed to know enough about the why of it before I could move on. How could I prevent it from happening again, if I didn't know why it happened in the first place?

He had no answers, or at least claimed he didn't. He always answered, "I don't know." Or "It just happened."

I would constantly pray that I would be given the answers about what I should do. Should I stay and try to work on this marriage or should I leave? These were some fairly simple, but very painful choices.

Do you sit and wait, not knowing what the end is going to be, or do you pick yourself up, dust yourself off, and start walking forward on your own journey? I certainly didn't ask for this to happen, but you begin to realize that you can only deal the best way you know how and hope for survival.

So often, I felt that I was in the way. If I just left, the two of them could be happy. I felt like a huge human wall separating them from being together. One night I told him how I felt and he cried. He asked me to please believe him that he wanted to spend the rest of his life with me.

I found myself making plans to take a leave of absence from work and leave town. I wouldn't tell anyone where I had gone. I would move around from motel to motel and finally settle in some little unknown town by the ocean. I might call one of my sons to let them know I was fine, but I would remain gone until I could heal from this trauma.

Through all this indecision, I finally made an appointment to talk to my doctor. I told her about the alcohol and she prescribed an anti-depressant and urged me to get an over the counter sleep aide, which I promptly did.

I know my finding these articles in his truck added to my level of insecurity. How could I trust this person? I would check his odometer before he left. Always watch which way he left for work and came home. I would frequently drive past her house and her place of employment to make sure he wasn't visiting her once again. I even had a device so that I could scan to see if he was using a cell phone to call her, as he often went down back on our property on some pretext or another.

One evening I had to go back to work, but I checked his odometer before I left. When I got back I found that there was 17 miles added. I asked him where he had been. He said he hadn't left, that he was there all evening. We went to bed, he feeling guilty about this new lie and me almost hating him for it. I did not sleep very much even with the help of the pills and wine. I was much too upset, thinking will this ever end?

The next morning I told him I knew he was lying but he still stuck with his story. Before he left I asked him if it was possible for a truck to put miles on by itself! When he arrived at work he called to tell me he had lied. That he was planning a surprise for me. He had gone to different travel agents to find out about taking a cruise. He said he found the surprise wasn't worth the lie.

That night he presented me with brochures of different cruise packages. I should have been pleased—but what stopped him from picking this information up through the day? I humored him, and we planned the cruise. At this time I very rarely told him of my insecurities and my suspicions. I just went with the flow and hoped for the best. My plan was to just watch and wait and leave when necessary. I was almost hoping he would see her again, so I could catch him and finally leave and end this insanity.

During the cruise I couldn't help but think, *Is this it? Is this his way of saying goodbye?* I was almost afraid for the cruise to be over. But much to my surprise, when we returned home, life went on as normally as it could under the circumstances.

Don't Rock the Boat!

Through all this time my son was going through a horrible custody battle with his ex-wife for the children. There was not an evening that went by that there would be some kind of a problem to cope with. Two different agencies performed psychological custody evaluations on both of the families along with inspecting our homes. The stress level of this added to the rest was off the charts.

Winter was fast approaching. My sister-in-law decided it was finally time to sell my mother-in-law's home. We immediately threw ourselves into cleaning, painting and some minor renovations. A week before Christmas the washing machine hose broke and the basement was flooded with over three feet of water.

The house was scheduled to be shown after Christmas, so we had to do our best to make everything presentable. While trying to dry out the basement through the next couple of days, my husband told me that he couldn't handle my insecurity anymore. He told me that he had been to see "her." He was worried about "her" and needed to think about who he wanted to spend his life with. Round three begins!

On New Year's Eve we talked some more. He said he was going to visit "her." I was sobbing as he left and then a calm peace overcame me and I began to realize our marriage was over. I started to think about my future without him. Oddly enough, I wasn't as frightened as I thought I would be. I merely accepted it and thought about how much planning there was for me to do.

He was gone maybe twenty minutes. When he returned he claimed she was "high" on something and probably didn't even know he was there. He stated he needed time to think and we could talk tomorrow about all of this. Happy New Year!

At this point in time my mother became aware of what was happening. I was talking to my sister on the phone, while my mother was visiting her. My sister said a few things to me that my mother had over-heard and she immediately thought my cancer was back and became quite upset.

A few days later my sister told me that she had to tell my mother what had been taking place in my life throughout the past year, because she knew something was wrong and was extremely agitated.

I waited a few weeks before I could talk to my mother. This was a hard thing for me to do, since I knew my mother thought the sun rose and set in my husband. I know the facts broke her heart, but she stated that she would be extremely supportive about whatever my decision would be.

Packing It Up and Leaving?

On New Year's Day I decided to take our Christmas tree down. Thinking I would be leaving soon, I gave no care about the way I packed the ornaments. I would be happy to put this entire mess well behind me. I needed to get far away from all the problems that I had been dealing with.

I began to experience heart palpitations a few days later and went to see my doctor. After an EKG she said that she thought I had a heart attack at some time in the past. She scheduled me for a stress test a few weeks later which turned out to be negative. The really weird thing about all of this was that I really didn't care if something was wrong with me.

The time I was told my cancer was back sent me over the edge and now when I was told I had a heart attack I was fine with it. I felt it was a means to the end of all this and I wouldn't even have to make plans now. After all hadn't I been hoping to drop out of site?

Through this period my husband told me once again that he wanted to continue his life with me. I had to question *Was this guilt talking because of my heart attack scare?*

I decided to make an appointment with a lawyer and a real estate agent to put the house on the market. I informed my husband that I would be the one making the decisions now and that's what I was going to do. He begged me to wait, claiming he couldn't live without me.

Thus began the healing! My energy was back and I was ready to spout outward. I was ready to face life again. As I let go of the anger, anxiety, pity and pain, I was lifted out of the grief cycle. I began to feel stronger and wiser from the painful lessons I had learned. The hate began to slowly seep from me.

That night I had a very vivid dream. Both my husband's parents, who had passed away, came to visit me. They were both crying and asked me to go with them. They took me back to our wedding. My husband and I were reciting our vows. Then we traveled back to their home and the three of us took a seat at their kitchen table; much like we use to when we visited them. They begged me to stay with their son and take care of him. That he wouldn't survive if I left. In my dream I promised I would. I woke up feeling extremely overwhelmed and somewhat at peace.

Later I realize that this dream may have been a way for my subconscious mind to tell me to do what my heart wanted to do. However, at that period of time, I took it quite seriously. I felt I should keep my promise!

Further Decision Makers

Our grandchildren's custody trial was scheduled to begin sometime in January and my son's lawyer told him it could jeopardize the custody case if his parents were to get a divorce at this time. He and the children were living with us and our divorcing and selling our home would be a major change in the children's life and therefore cause them instability.

So I found myself back to the drawing board. I took the attitude that I was leaving as soon as I could. He decided he wanted to spend his life with me. I trusted him less than ever before. Was he staying because of the custody?

Life seemed to go on without too much turmoil. The custody case came and both parents were given shared custody for the time being, but a later trial was set for September. More waiting!

Things finally appeared to be much better. Was there a chance for us to reconcile? I became more at ease. I didn't feel it necessary to check on my husband's every move. I stopped traveling by "her" house and place of employment. Yes, things were finally improving. I simply stopped giving this whole sordid ordeal any energy. I needed my energy to heal and plan a new life if it should become necessary.

Spring arrived and we were definitely on the road to recovery. We talked about one day renewing our vows, perhaps taking a trip or two. Also, some long range plans—after retirement, etc. but I still didn't feel like I had a lot of faith to see any of those plans fulfilled. I didn't feel comfortable planning this great future we frequently talked about. I knew I was strong enough to make it on my own. It seemed appealing to never have to wonder if "she" was still in his life or on his mind. How peaceful my life could be if I chose to walk down that other path by myself!

Summer seemed to bring us closer together. We were working together on renovating the house and remodeling his old car for resale. I was beginning to really feel happy again and yes, even more secure.

Oh, there were still moments of doubt. Maybe he was just waiting to finish remodeling his car before he leaves. He can't leave now! The car is in a hundred pieces all over the cellar. Perhaps I'll help him finish it and he can leave sooner.

So many dark thoughts kept going through my brain! I couldn't seem to shake the feeling something was still not right between us.

In the Ring to Be Beat Up Again!

Father's day arrived and I was feeling sad that our sons hadn't thought to call their dad to wish him a happy Father's Day. I felt that would give him the message that they were still quite upset with him.

My husband actually seemed indifferent about this and somewhat pre-occupied. I began to notice his actions. I happened to witness him standing beside his open truck door, he looked around to make sure no one was watching and stooped down and took something from under the truck seat. He promptly put it in his pocket. He then told me he was going down in the field to cut grass.

By this time my suspicion level was about 100 percent. I guessed immediately that he had taken a phone from his truck. After he had gone down into the field, I listened for the lawn mower to shut off and it did. My instinct told me if I went down into the field I would find some interesting things out. I took the other tractor and went down. When he saw me it became obvious he had something to hide.

I looked him over and saw no sign of a phone in his pocket. Upon scanning the area, I noticed his shirt hanging in a tree near-by. I began to walk toward the tree knowing he didn't want me to. He instantly took my arm and steered me to another area in the yard to show me raspberries. Raspberries! When was he ever interested in raspberries! I humored him and then started back to the tree. We were talking and I knew he didn't want me by that tree as he kept positioning himself between it and me.

I told him I would take his shirt up to the house. He strongly objected! I knew then that I found what I was looking for. I turned to go, then abruptly turned and grabbed his shirt from the tree. When he tried to take it from me, the phone fell out of his pocket onto the ground.

I refer to this as D-day number 3. The anger rose up in me like an erupting volcano. I began yelling about how the two of them are probably having a good laugh about how gullible I have been and what a fool I am. He kept saying that he could explain.

I told him, "No more explaining, I was leaving!"

I left the tractor in the field and ran up through the yard. He was right behind me. I knew he was having a difficult time walking because he had injured his back, but I simply didn't care. I wanted him to hurt as bad as I was hurting.

We were both out of breath and crying when we got inside the house. He kept saying how he could explain and of course I was thoroughly disgusted with his explanations. I had heard enough!

He began to tell me it was "her" phone. She had given it to him so he could call her to find out how she was. He confessed that he had also been by to see "her," but not frequently. He swore nothing had happened when he visited. They were short visits—he just needed to keep in contact to see that she was doing alright.

My thought was, *how many times is this going to happen?* Maybe never again, because it seems he can't put "her" from his life. I again tell him I must leave. I will go and live with my sister or move to another state. I will take a leave of absence, until he moves his things out of the house. I tell him to please go down and live with "her."

He cried some more—"I can't live without you, he claims!"

I reply, "Well, obviously you can't live without her either."

I tell him I will not under any circumstances be his "other

women." She may have been alright with that title, but I have too much respect for myself to play that game! Again, I tell him to please go live with her, it's over between us.

He began to cry again and say sarcastically what a great father he is and how proud his father would be of him. He tells me he knows now that he can live without her and he promises me he will. I am doubtful.

I tell him he is selfish to keep us both strung along, thinking he loves us both. Does he not realize "she" is full of hope because of his renewed contact? How very hurtful this is to her and what kind of person would do that to someone they profess to love. I explained that any contact with her gives her false hope. If he doesn't want a future with her, can't he see how mean that is? I call him a "cake-eater"!

I then told him that if I am to stay it is truth time. Time for the answers I so desperately needed.

I asked, "Why did this affair happen?"

He replied, "I don't know, perhaps it was not feeling needed, a mid-life crisis, someone paying attention to me and making me feel important."

My next question was, "How long have you been seeing, talking to her this time?"

He stated, "Since last January, just to make sure she was alright. Nothing happened, the visits were short and not that frequent."

I then asked him who pays for her phone, since she is so destitute. He said, "I don't know, probably her daughter."

"Are you helping her with her bills or giving her more money?" I asked.

He replied, "No."

I then asked him to tell me about how they met and how the relationship evolved to become emotional and physical. He said that he met her in the doughnut shop and she was very friendly. They talked about her two bad marriages and a lot of other things. She invited him to go out to have a sandwich with her and he refused, but she kept insisting. He said he knew it was wrong, but finally went. He added that they went out to eat a few times then they began to meet at her house.

I asked him, "Did you feel good about yourself at the time?"

He answered, "No. I hated myself and what this would do to you if you found out.

"Why did you tell me when you did?," I asked. "Was it because you waited until your mother passed away and she wouldn't find out? If so you are fooling yourself because both of your parents already know."

He replied, "I told you when I did because 'she' was pressuring me to get a divorce and marry her. I hated myself and couldn't live with myself anymore knowing what I was doing to you and our family. The lies and pretense were killing me!"

I told him the only way I would stay is that he must write her a brief letter telling her it is over. That he loves his wife and he will not be in any contact with her ever again. He agreed to do this.

He wrote the letter, which I read. He delivered the letter to her house along with her phone at a time when he was sure she was not there. Again, I am trusting his word! Should I? This question plagued me daily for a month or two.

I traveled out for state with my mother to visit my son and his family. My son just accepted an appointment in a large church as assistant pastor and this would be his first sermon. For some reason I didn't feel anxious about leaving my husband and cared little at this time about trusting him. My feeling was that if he contacted her again, I would certainly find out in good time. I had the attitude—go for it! Just try it and *you won't even see my dust!*

My son was very hurt that his dad did not come to support him. He made the comment that it probably gave him a great opportunity to see his girlfriend while I was gone. He also told me that if his dad continued to see "her," there would be no way that he would ever see his grandchildren again. He further stated that this is not the person who raised him. His father taught him to respect your wife and the father he knew had high morals. He said his father has turned into a stranger!

I left my son's home feeling upset. Was I completely wrong to trust this stranger who was trying hard to act like my husband? My thoughts were often sporadic during this period. One day I would feel he is on his own and what ever he decides he will have to live with. I simply didn't care because I really looked forward to the peace of leaving it all behind me.

Then within hours and sometimes minutes I would find myself doubting his sincerity and needing to prove his unfaithfulness once again. I sometimes went out of my way to try to catch him at her house or assume when the phone was busy at his place of work that he was indeed talking to her.

I recall telling him during this period, that it is very important that he is honest about all things. If he even thinks he needs to talk to her, I would like him to tell me before he does so. However, if I find out after the fact that there has been any kind of contact, I would not only end our marriage but also our friendship. There would be no more chances!

The Visit

One day while I had been out shopping, I went past "her" house. I noticed she had a brand new car! Well, so much for the story about her losing everything! As I drove past I had this overwhelming feeling to turn around and go back and talk to her.

I knocked on her door. She answered. I introduced myself and told her I thought it was time we met. Her response was "Oh, my God!"

I asked her if she would kindly come out on the porch and talk to me briefly. I wished her no harm. She said her grandchildren were visiting, and she was on the phone "talking to my husband" at the moment but would be right out.

I sat and waited while I tried to calm my erratic heart beat. When she joined me, the first thing I thought to ask was "Did you receive a letter from my husband and did you get your phone back"?

Her reply was "No" to both questions.

She asked me what he had been telling me lately. She said that he lies about everything and she was sure he had been lying to me for quite awhile. She stated they were engaged, and she showed me her diamond. They would be getting married next year. I told her we planned to renew our vows.

She told me how he had thrown his wedding ring in the creek beside her house last year. I told her his wedding ring had been destroyed years ago in an accident.

Through our talking I began to believe her about his lying. It

46

was hard to determine if she was lying or not. She painted my husband out to be a compulsive liar, who would do anything to get his way. Certainly not the person I have lived with all these years. But then, hadn't he become a stranger by doing things I never would have thought possible?

When she began to tell me that our sons knew her and were anxious to have her in the family, as well as my sister-in-laws, I realized she was lying. She also claimed to know my mother-in-law and was also well liked by her. Wow! Big lie there!

Much more was said that day. I must confess that I got angry but I am sure it didn't surface. She claimed the affair was going on much longer than he originally confessed. Also, he had told her that we hadn't slept together in over ten years. I assured her that was not the case. We both admitted to each other that we were currently having sexual relations with him.

She said that he would have left me a long time ago but was concerned about my health and my son losing the custody of the children.

She then told me she had something to tell me that would really hurt me. She proceeded to tell me that after he had told me about the affair, he had given her money. I could tell she thought this was news to me. I told her, I knew about that and it wasn't really "his" money, but rather left to me by my aunt. That we had to pay a large amount of tax on it, so we could help her out. I knew this revelation hurt her, but I really didn't care.

I began to realize it was time to say goodbye. I went over to her, gave her a hug and said, "I am sorry. At one point in the past I really hated you and I am sorry for that."

She asked could we keep in contact, so we could continue to compare notes to determine what he was up to.

I said, "No, that isn't a good idea."

I did ask her to please not let him know that I had been by to visit her. I would rather talk to him about it myself. I explained how suicidal he was and said I didn't want to cause that kind of problem again.

She stated, "Oh, he was never going to hurt himself."

As I was getting into my car she asked if we would see each other again. I said, "No, probably not, but if we do, I hope it isn't at his funeral."

The visit did two things for me. First, it made me realize who this "other person" was, and gave me a brief view of what she was like.

Secondly, I exercised all those demons that had been haunting me. I was no longer afraid of her or what she could possibly do to me.

Also, now she could also put a face to "his wife" and realize I was a real human being with feelings. The strange thing I realized was that she made me feel like the intruder in their life.

She did stress, before I left, that it was probably a good thing for me to leave him, so he could get on with his life. It was almost like she felt she knew him better than I did and was in fact his wife for all those years. I found that to be really freaky.

Will the Honest Person Please Come Forward

I didn't realize how very upset this visit caused me to feel until my trip home. A thousand thoughts raced through my mind. Is my husband a compulsive liar or is she? Well, I went this far to get to the bottom of the story; I thought I would continue until I had the whole story. Upon arriving home, I promptly called my husband and told him I wasn't feeling very well, could he please come home. I was so worried that she would contact him before I did and tell him of my visit. I needed to see his face when he heard that I had been to visit "her" and relate what had been told to me.

He was home within one half hour. I told him where I had been and what had transpired. He wasn't upset that I had been to see her and offered to go back down to her house to clear up the lies she had told me. I refused because her grandchildren were visiting her and I thought that would be really awkward for us all. I look back now and wish I had done just that.

The next work day, she called my husband at work and was very angry that I had been to see her. She called me his whore. She advised him that she and her daughter would be at our home that evening to ruin our lives, like he ruined hers. She stressed that the only way she wouldn't come to our house was if he came to see her directly after work and told her to her face he didn't love her.

He came right home after work and told me about all of this.

He was really concerned that they might visit us that evening, but they never showed up. I knew they wouldn't and I now had a different idea about what she was really like. This didn't seem to be the type of person my husband would love. I almost felt sorry for the feelings and lost years he had spent in her company. But I know in my heart we all have lessons to be taught and perhaps that was a part of his schooling or perhaps his life with me was part of his schooling. We may never know.

Time passed, not necessarily easy time. My older son making great strides building his new home. I found myself doing what I could to help with his children; sometimes using the nail gun to help them nail the flooring, and other times helping move things. There are meals to prepare to feed the hungry crew, washing clothes and at times my grandchildren wish to stay at our home because there really isn't too much for them to do at the building site.

The sad part of all this is that my husband is now suffering from excruciating back pain. What started out as bad back pain has now gone to debilitating pain, with need for an operation. The operation was not successful but led to worse pain then he previously had. He has not worked since the surgery, six months ago. His neurosurgeon has left his practice and moved out of state. We have already traveled to three other surgeons and not had very much help. We are waiting to visit a doctor in another state to find out about a new procedure called endoscopic lumbar surgery. We are really counting on this!

My thoughts now run amuck! I hate so much seeing him in this kind of pain. Some days I find it is worse seeing him in pain than knowing he had "a girlfriend." One has to put things into perspective and realize there are so many people worse off than you.

I began to realize that one reason his affair happened was that he wasn't feeling needed. WOW! Now when he is needed he can't do too much about it. Irony indeed! Then he tries to relate to me how difficult it is to sleep at night because of the pain.

I just smile and tell him "Yes, I understand how difficult it is to not be able to sleep because of pain."

Yes, our pain was very different, but it was pain nonetheless.

Then there was the fact that he found he was unable to trust doctors to help him. He questioned me "Do you know what it's like to not be able to trust people."

"Yes", I reply, "I do."

I once tried to tell him I think seeing him in pain like this hurts me so bad and now I know it is much worse than knowing he had "a friend." I told him to look at those dark spots of his life that he never thought he could get over and compare it with this.

He simply stated, "I want to put the past behind me. Couldn't we do that? I am tired of it all." I felt scolded and vowed to never speak of it all again.

I realize in my heart that this is not the end of this story. She is not the kind of person to let him go so easily. I still find myself poised upon a fence—with one wing in the air ready to fly if need be.

I have gotten to a place where I am much stronger, I like myself again, and need to put my energy to the work to accomplish what I was sent on the earth to do. I could be ready in a minute to fly to that safe haven and put this all behind me and not have to worry about whom is seeing whom any longer.

This has already taken up too much of my time and energy. I have learned a lot about human nature. I have become less trustful and somewhat harder. I am not as prone to tears as I used to be. Are they all gone? Maybe it's because I am still on the anti-anxiety medicine. I am not sure when I dare stop my medicine. I don't want to go back to that dark place again, it isn't very fun.

I have decided to focus my future on thinking good thoughts about people and trying to help them. There was a period of perhaps six months that I went on the internet to help sites for people who have been betrayed. I am not sure I helped anyone there, but I received a font of information and incite. When it became depressing to see how prevalent affairs are in this age I knew it was time to move on.

I also began to realize that when I had spent any time on the marriage betrayal sites, I was giving more energy to my own betrayal. This would usually follow with my need to talk to my husband and look for more answers—answers that neither one of us will ever have. When actually the only question I need answered for the rest of my life is: Will he continue to be faithful to me and finally leave her behind?

The moving on and the forgiveness are only a small part of this horribly long process for me. There are so many phases to evolve through after a betrayal of this kind. At this point in time, if I am not fooling myself, I would like to think I am seeing the light at the end of the tunnel. It has been two and a half years since "the confession." I would love to say everything is just wonderful, but it isn't.

My younger son told me that a lot of times when a marriage has gone through what ours did it becomes much better than it ever was. He said it was like the prize vessel being broken, it is in a lot of pieces, but it has emitted sweet perfume. There are some definite good changes. However, I would not wish for anyone to go through such a heart rendering betrayal.

A betrayal of this kind is similar to destroying the home you have with your family, your life and the trust anyone might have in you. It has the ability to also destroy the desire to live for all involved. A large price to pay for delightful deception!

If you are reading this and having thoughts of going forward with "that other person," you need to consider the long range domino effect of your actions. This kind of pain lasts for weeks, months and years. It destroys your life, the lives of not only your spouse but your entire family and the family of that other person. If you are bound and determined to walk down this path, do yourself and everyone else a favor, leave the marriage. Walk away, end the marriage before you bring this amount of devastation on people who have done nothing to you but love you, care for you and be there for you.

I question, "Should I continue spending time in a relationship that is doomed to end at some point in the future?" After reading this, you may think the answer is no.

My husband and I continue to communicate about this. I know it pains him to talk about it and I feel he still harbors deep feelings for this other person. I can't be certain if this will ever change. I do know I will keep my word and leave if any contact happens again. You see I must continue to like myself and maintain my high morals.

This is my life, all of my life, as opposed to 'only' sexual betrayal, and, finally at the end, even deep emotional betrayal too. Yet this is the story of my life, and I decided eventually that I had to continue that story, that this wasn't the end. That I could continue writing, if only in my heart.

I have found life is about choices and it is better to not try to understand why people make the choices they do. We are only accountable for ourselves and not anyone else.

We are all here on this life's journey to become better people. We must forgive and move on no matter how hard. When our life is over can we say, "I did the best I could with those people God was good enough to let me come in contact with."

Thank you God for those lessons to move onward as a better person.

Go with the grace of God.

Printed in the United States
25151LVS00002B/40-69

9 781413 751550